Serendipity Says

to know me

is

to love me

written by
Marcia Trimble

illustrated by
Susi Grell

Images Press – Los Altos Hills, California

ACKNOWLEDGMENT:
Special thanks to Chris Putland for his generosity in permitting the use of his character design of Serendipity.

Published by Images Press

Publisher's Cataloging-in-Publication
(Provided by Quality Books, Inc.)

Trimble, Marcia.
    Serendipity says to know me is to love me / written by Marcia Trimble ;
illustrated by Susi Grell. -- 1st ed.
    p. cm.
    Includes bibliographical references.
    LCCN: 99-97128
    ISBN: 1-891577-77-8 (hbk)
    Summary: Malinda Martha enjoys the story of a sea serpent named Serendipity, who has been turned into the force behind the tides, and who proceeds to teach the girl to appreciate the unexpected discoveries of life.

    1. Tides--Juvenile fiction. 2. Serendipity--Juvenile fiction. 3. Seashore--Juvenile fiction.
I. Grell, Susi. II. Title.

PZ7.T7352Se 2000   [E]
                QBI99-1862

10 9 8 7 6 5 4 3 2 1

Text was set in Verdana, Spumoni, Lemonade, and Pepita.
Book design by MontiGraphics

Printed in Hong Kong by South China Printing Co. (1988) Ltd. on totally chlorine-free Nymolla Matte Art paper.

This book is dedicated to Malinda Martha and everyone else everywhere whose eyes are open for the discoveries and surprises of life... and recognizes them when they see them.   M.T.

To my loving parents, Helga and Karl, who mean the world to me, and to James, who makes it spin 'round...love always, Susi

The old books at "Doc's Box" smelled of the sea.

The sea breezes of summer
scented their pages
as Malinda Martha looked for the treasures
between their covers.

She spotted a sea serpent
with a very long name.
"Ser-en-dip-i-ty," she said.
"Serendipity,
   you have a very long name,
      and a very long *tail*...and
         a very short **tale**, too!"
            She giggled
               as her eyes
                  slithered
                     into his

very

short

tale.

One day a long time ago,
Old Sol, the sun,
cast a topsy-turvy spell
on a sea serpent
and the man-in-the-moon.

Old Methodical,

as the man-in-the-moon was called,

dared to slip between Old Sol and the earth,

casting a shadow

that turned day into night.*

* Solar eclipse

Old Sol caught Old Methodical blocking his rays and punished him by taking away his greatest joy...

his power to rule the tides.

Alas! Old Sol spied Serendipity, the sea serpent, frolicking in the waves, showing off his strong back, his wavy body, and his *long tail.* "The perfect specimen!" he thought.

And with that, Old Sol turned Serendipity into a tidal serpent.

Old Methodical
has been sleeping
ever since...
while Serendipity
rises and falls,
rises and falls.

Twice every day,
Serendipity slithers far up onto the shore.
He sputters as he spits out stones
and groans when sand sticks
to the roof of his mouth...
as he swallows the sand sculptures.

Twice every day, as he slips away,

he swishes the beach with his tail

and scatters sea life along the shore.

He yearns for the time

when he can return to his kingdom

at the bottom of the sea...

when he can swim with his grand-sea serpents once more.

To this day, Serendipity is waiting

for a child to break the spell...

a child who loves him

and understands him.

THE END

All night, Malinda Martha dreamed about Serendipity...
imagining that she was the child...

and in the morning,
she ran to the beach
with images of Serendipity
still in her head.

She picked up flat wet stones that glistened like gems in the sunlight and sent them skimming across the water. She liked to watch the stones skip and spin shapes that shimmer…and spread out… and steal away. She pretended the stones were stealing away to Serendipity's kingdom in the sea.

"Serendipity must be out," she said.

"Serendipity rises and falls
with the tick of the clock,"
said Daddy.

"He slithers toward my castle
as if he can't stop...
not even at my wall of flat rock,"
chimed in Malinda Martha.

"Serendipity doesn't really like stones,"
said Mother.

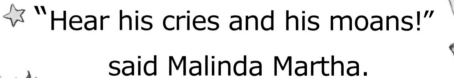 "Hear his cries and his moans!"

said Malinda Martha.

"He's not very well

'cause he's caught in that spell.

Who will break the spell?"

"Time will tell," said Daddy.

"Time will tell."

"I like playing the Serendipity game,"
said Malinda Martha. "I want to break the spell!
I hope Serendipity left a clue."

"You can't look for Serendipity,
but he can look for you,"
said Daddy.

"He comes when
you're not looking,
but you'll know when
he comes," said Mother,
joining in.

"But I want to understand him.
I want to look for clues,"
said Malinda Martha.

"Look! Serendipity scatters sea life
along the shore.

Sea shells and starfish and
seaweed move in and out."

"A clue wouldn't move in and out!"
said Mother.

"Serendipity spits out stones," said Malinda Martha, "stones to skip, and stones that splash...and tumble...and toss about."

"A clue wouldn't tumble and toss about!" said Daddy.

"Serendipity swishes the beach with his tail. He  leaves smooth sand...but sand patterns change.
I know! A clue wouldn't change!" chanted Malinda Martha.

"Serendipity swallows sand sculptures! Like my sand castle."
Malinda Martha sighed. "Maybe Serendipity swallowed the clue."

"You can't look for clues," said Daddy. "You can't look for Serendipity."

"Then I'll look for the key
to his kingdom,"
said Malinda Martha.

She giggled
at that idea!

"I've got it!

I'll send Serendipity
a letter in a bottle," she said.
"I'll tell him about my discovery."

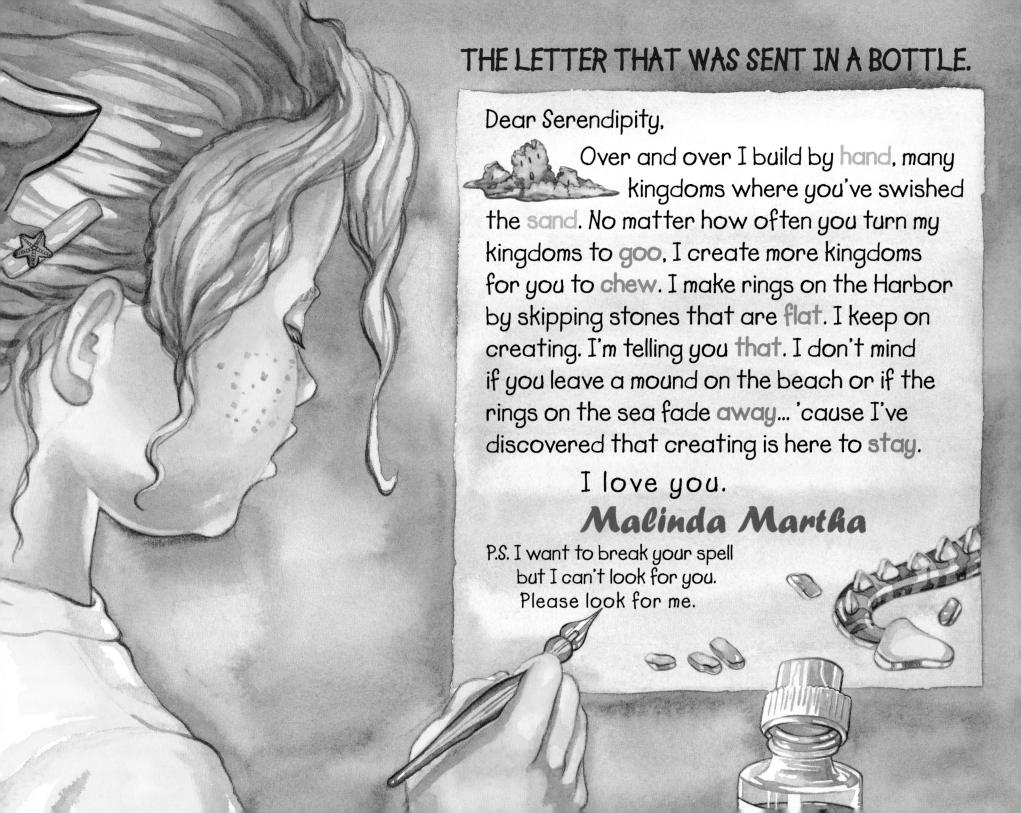

THE LETTER THAT WAS SENT IN A BOTTLE.

Dear Serendipity,

Over and over I build by hand, many kingdoms where you've swished the sand. No matter how often you turn my kingdoms to goo, I create more kingdoms for you to chew. I make rings on the Harbor by skipping stones that are flat. I keep on creating. I'm telling you that. I don't mind if you leave a mound on the beach or if the rings on the sea fade away... 'cause I've discovered that creating is here to stay.

I love you.

Malinda Martha

P.S. I want to break your spell
but I can't look for you.
Please look for me.

It was the last day of summer vacation,
time to pack up for the 8 p.m. ferry crossing.

No more walks along the beach.
No more summer sunsets.
No more skipping stones.
No more Serendipity game.

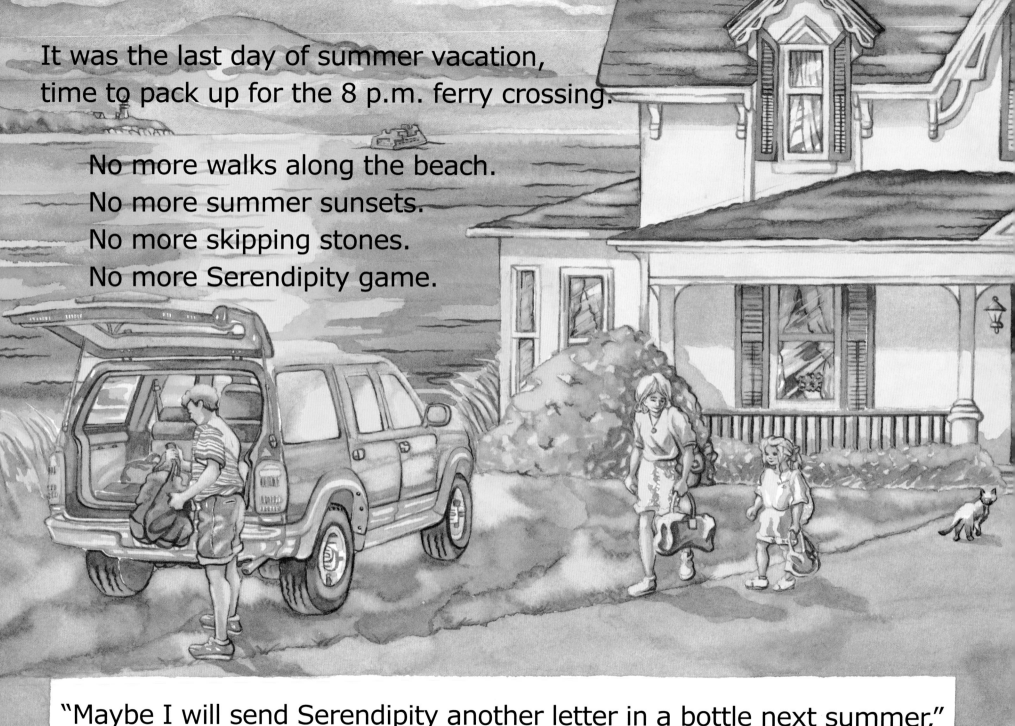

"Maybe I will send Serendipity another letter in a bottle next summer," said Malinda Martha. "But I still hope that Serendipity will look for me."

Malinda Martha
ran to the sand
to find one smooth flat stone
to slip in her backpack.
She wanted to take home
a piece of summer.

She glanced out at the waves.

She was imagining a bottle drifting
far away to a kingdom in the sea...
when she saw a bottle floating toward her!
"Oh, no! My bottle's floating back,"
she cried out.

She grabbed the bottle
and pulled out the cork.
"Something is in the bottle!"
she exclaimed.

She unrolled the paper and
gazed at the message.

Malinda Martha burst into a smile!

Rhymes rolled through her head like waves rolling onto the beach.

I lost my castle and I lost my rings. I was looking for a way to save those things when it dawned on me... I can't lose creativity. Then...I was looking for a skipping stone to save when a bottle with a message washed ashore upon a wave. Keep your eyes open, the message said. Discoveries may be hiding on the path ahead.

I was looking for a stone
but...I found something else
instead. Wow! It was just like
Daddy said it would be.
Serendipity crept up on me.

Malinda Martha skipped
along, clapping a jingle.

"Serendipity, Serendipity*,
I'm not looking.
I'm not looking.
I'm not looking for a clue.
I can never look for you.
I'll be looking for something else
when you come into view."

* Making a fortunate discovery
  while looking for something else.

"Old Sol has set Serendipity free," said Daddy, "and in gratitude for his service has decreed that **Serendipity's spirit** will be known henceforth as *'the surprises that happen when you're not looking for them, when you're looking for something else'*... and in Serendipity's honor will be named after him!"

Daddy winked!

"And...that is why the fortunate discoveries that you make when you aren't looking for them are called **'serendipity'**."

And...from that day to this,

Serendipity has been known in his kingdom
at the bottom of the sea as

"the sea serpent with a special name
and an endearing spirit".

Old Methodical
is awake.
Serendipity
is swimming free!
The tides are
on schedule again.